DROWN IN YOU

A DARK SAPPHIC SHORT STORY

J ROSE

WILTED ROSE PUBLISHING

FOREWORD

Dear Reader,

This story may be short and smutty, but it is suffused in darkness. As always, I write from my soul about the things I care about.

LGBTQ+ rights are something I am incredibly passionate about. As a queer, bisexual woman, defending our right to exist isn't something to be debated. Our world is far from equal and there is still so much work to be done.

1/8 of all LGBTQ+ individuals in the UK have attempted suicide.

For every last person out there questioning their identity, feeling overwhelmed, confused, alone, lost — you are not alone.

Your life matters.

For UK readers, here are some places that can help.

www.stonewall.org.uk

www.lgbt.foundation

www.galop.org.uk

I know what it's like to want to disappear. There are so many people here to listen and help.

Samaritans – Call 116 123

Text 'Shout' to 85258

Papyrus Suicide Prevention – Call 0800 0684141

I'm not a professional. This short story isn't a self-help guide. I learned to deal with my trauma by writing it all out.

I found hope.

I hope you do to.

Love always, J Rose x

TRIGGER WARNING

This sapphic short story includes content that may be triggering for some readers including suicide, self-harm, physical and sexual abuse.

There are also scenes of consensual non-consent, gun play, blood play, BDSM, asphyxiation, orgasm denial and edge play.

Reader discretion is advised.

CHAPTER
ONE
ARIEL

MY EXCITED FOOTSTEPS are lit by the gleam of moonshine. Dappling light across cobbled stones and chiselled crucifixes, it douses the thick blanket of night in shades of hope.

I didn't bring a flashlight this time. I don't want to risk waking my parents up in the vicarage across the street. Pain still thrums through my body from last night's beating.

My father, the esteemed Pastor Kane, caught me drinking communion wine I had stolen from the church. I like the feeling it gives me—confidence, strength, power. It emboldened me to take the rusty scissors to my long, angelic blonde hair.

Both parents gaped when they saw me.

My hair was freshly shorn and eyes lit with devilish defiance.

Father made me kneel by the open fireplace beneath the watchful gaze of the Father, Son and Holy Spirit. He read from the Bible before beating me until his knuckles cracked and bled.

I can still hear his sermon echoing in my concussed head.

Please, Lord Above.

Spare our daughter your mercy.

Deliver her from evil and temptation.

After racing past gravestones and statues of saints I can never hope to live up to, I reach the quiet cocoon of the church. St

Lucien's is the crown jewel of Darkling Heath. The rest of the sleepy village revolves around this point. Every last soul has pledged their allegiance to my father and his congregation.

We live by a strict code of conduct.

Any incursions upon this are swiftly punished.

Even if you're the pastor's daughter.

The side entrance to the church is still unlocked after I tampered with it this morning in preparation. Using nothing but touch and memory, I feel my way into the darkness. Icy coldness bites into my skin, freezing every limb but failing to douse the lion's heart burning in my chest.

I've had to keep my distance in public to minimise suspicion. Nobody can ever know about what we have, but it's her birthday today. We're both sixteen years old. I've been waiting for this moment for a long time. We could finally make it out there, in the real world, with nothing but each other.

"Leah? Where are you?"

Her voice calls back in a sweet, otherworldly tenor.

"Over here. Under the altar."

The flare of a match breaks the darkness. Smoothing my plain linen dress, I approach the altar, my patent Mary Jane's tapping against the stone floor. Leah is crouched underneath, hidden by the thick, cotton cloth embroidered with the crucifix in glimmering gold thread.

I stare down at her. My Mary Magdalene, the key to my true self. I'm wrapped in layers of subterfuge and false beliefs. I put on a good show, speak when spoken to, recite the scripture with utmost perfection.

But not with her.

Around Leah, I'm as broken as I feel.

"Happy birthday!"

"What happened to you?" she gasps.

"It's nothing, really."

"You're covered in bruises!"

Leah's fingers cover her naturally blushed lips. Her hair is long and curling in the most indistinct shade of mousy brown. It compliments her slim, bird-like features and wide, doe eyes that lure you in without warning.

She wears an identical dress to me, dyed the exact shade of a summer's sky, complimenting her unblemished, milky skin. No bruises mark her body. There's no malice or hatred in her eyes.

She's pure, unspoiled, dutiful, and *mine*.

"Pastor Kane caught me again," I admit hoarsely.

When I slide beneath the altar to join her, the single candle lights the concern creasing up her delicate features. I reach out without thinking, stroking a digit over the frown marring her eyebrows.

"You shouldn't steal, it isn't allowed," Leah murmurs.

"That's exactly why I do it, wildflower."

Her frown deepens. "You want to get in trouble?"

"Don't you?"

"Of course not. I want to serve Pastor Kane and the church."

I can't suppress my scoff. "Were you serving him when my tongue was inside your wet, pious pussy the other night?"

The colour drains from Leah's face.

It hurts me to do it, but I have to treat her this way.

I don't want the world to break her before I can.

"That isn't fair," she whispers. "I can't do this anymore. The lying, sneaking around, hiding from my father. We should just tell everyone about us. They'll understand, I know they will."

"You're so fucking naive, Leah."

"Hey!" she snaps.

"What? You can't handle the truth?"

"You're being mean."

There's a bonfire brightening her dull blue eyes. They look like the limitless expanse of a lake, muddied and clouded with lies. Only I can spark the flame that burns within her. Others see an empty vessel for the church and all its backwards beliefs, but my wildflower is so much more.

"Your father is no better than mine," I say harshly, watching the pain etch across her face. "He doesn't know any better than to hate what the church tells him to. You know it's a sin, two women being together. They will never accept our relationship."

Tears gather and roll down her cheeks. Instinctively, I reach out with a single fingertip and swipe the moisture. Leah watches as I lick the bead of salt, stealing her sadness for myself. I'll lock her soul in a box and bury it at the bottom of the ocean if it protects what we have.

"Let's run," I blurt.

Her eyes grow even wider. "What?"

"We've talked about it before. I have some cash and a bus map, we could be on the other side of England by tomorrow night. They never have to know where we went."

Her teeth bite into her bottom lip, raw from anxious chewing. Leah is the ice to my fire, a cool compress to the sweaty forehead of the delirious. Every step she takes is carefully considered, keeping in line with the strictness of our upbringing. She's a textbook perfectionist.

Me on the other hand? I went the other way. The harder my parents pushed, the further I strayed from the holy path. For each beating and lesson, I rebelled even harder. I won't stop, not now.

We deserve to live the lives we want to. Nobody should be forced to be someone they're not. This world loves to tell us who we can and can't love, like it's that easy to simply choose.

"We can't run," Leah responds. "I won't leave my father behind, I'm all he has left now. Just stay with me. We can be together just like we have been. Nothing has to change."

Disappointment sours my stomach. With words alone, she's sent the hope steeling my spine up in flames. I can't go back to that vicarage. Not again. This time, when my father beats the Devil out of me, I'm scared he will break something far more precious and irreplaceable.

"Why won't you fight for me?"

Leah flinches. "I'm not giving up on us."

"You already did."

Finding my feet, the surrounding church spins on its axis. It feels like the rug has been pulled from beneath my feet, leaving me to fall to the consumption of the abyss. Before I can run, a hand tugs on mine. Leah pleads me with her eyes, abandoning the safety of her hiding place.

If only she would show such bravery in front of the world.

If only she were willing to risk it all in the name of love.

"Please, Ariel. Don't go."

"Why should I stay? They'll kill me. You know that, right? One day, I'll step too far out of line. I'd rather end up like Mary-Sue than be sacrificed in the name of some loveless God I don't believe in."

I'm startled by the hand that strikes me. Pain blooms across my left cheek, hot beneath my palm. Leah's chest is heaving with each furious breath, the life back in her eyes. She looks like she wants to hit me again. Over and over, fists on blood, fear on regret, until I bend to her will.

"Don't you dare bring her into this," she seethes. "Mary-Sue was my friend before she hung herself. I won't lose another one. Haven't I lost enough already? You want to join that long list?"

I know she's thinking of her mother just by looking at her face. Mrs Bethel was a kind woman, much like her daughter. She would tend to the elderly in the village, manage the collection during our weekly services, even bake apple pies for the families that make up St Lucien's congregation.

You would think that Pastor Kane could overlook what happened, given the love and generosity that suffused the very air she breathed. It did nothing to alleviate his wrath when Mrs Bethel was discovered having an affair with Mr Holsten, the baker's brother.

None of us have seen her since. Just like Mary-Sue, she left without a goodbye. That's when the waterfall of hope flowing through Leah dried up. No amount of meticulous pretending will bring her back.

"I'm sorry," I offer quietly.

But I've unleashed the beast, and Leah isn't done. Her nails leave bloodied, crescent grooves in my arms as she pulls me back to her. Our chests collide, one full chest against another that is flat and petite. My hands weave into her long hair without thinking, angling her lips up.

Leah holds her breath. "Don't be sorry. Stay."

"I can't. This place...it's killing me. More and more every day."

"Then let me hold you together. I won't let you drown."

Her lips smash against mine with the full force of the Lord's almighty wrath. She plays a clever game, this fallen angel. Prancing around like a deer in headlights, full of all the right words. But in private? I see the anger that thrums in her veins.

The injustice.

The hatred.

The need for vengeance.

She tries to hide it, but we're the same on many levels. Nobody else makes her feel as alive as me, and she's the only thing that makes me want to keep going. That's the power I hold over her—that ripe, juicy heart beating in her chest belongs to me. I won't leave without her.

Backing Leah up against the altar, my mouth attacks hers in a torrent of frenzied need. Her tongue is like warm velvet in my mouth, claiming my soul over and over again. Each stroke is a brand on my skin, blazoned for the world to see if only she could find the courage.

Squeezing her hips, I break the kiss and fall to my knees. Her head is thrown back already, legs spread as my hands glide over the soft fuzz covering her skin. Holding her dress to her belly with one hand, I gently stroke her glistening cunt with the other. She's soaked as always, permanently ready for me.

"Ariel—"

"Yes?" I growl back.

"Please..."

"Please what, wildflower? I thought I was being mean, huh?"

Her hips undulate, pressing her wet mound to my lips. I know what she wants. Servicing my girl is the only thing in this damned world that I'm good for. Swiping my tongue against the seam of her pussy lips, I lap at the expanse of heat gathered between her legs.

"Oh God," she mewls. "More!"

Just as her whimpering begins to build, the sound of heavy footsteps breaks the bubble around us. I realise too late to hide or run. On a sick, twisted level, part of me is glad to find my father watching us with brimstone in his gaze.

I drop Leah's dress to cover her nakedness, not bothering to wipe the gleam of moisture from my lips. I want him to see us like this. The people we are, deep down, beyond his hateful prejudices.

"My daughter," he proclaims with bitter grandeur. "The whore."

I shove Leah behind me. "Father—"

"It's Pastor Kane to you, little slut. Kneel."

A snowstorm brews beneath my skin until I'm full-body shivering. Leah tries to whisper something, urging me to let her take the fall, but I shove her backwards until she collides with the altar again. Each step towards my father echoes through the church like the signed seal on a death warrant.

"Kneel," he repeats.

I stare into his bottomless brown eyes, framed with soft smile lines and the perfect curls of a swoon-worthy model. He's a handsome exterior printed across a toxic spirit. I see the blow coming a mile off, matching the handprint already inflicted by the girl I'm protecting.

I do the only thing I can do.

Not kneel. Not submit.

Not shrink to fit his ideals and principles.

I hit him back with every bit of hatred I feel for this church. Pastor Kane stumbles, his coal-black robes swirling like smoke, as he cups the reddened flesh of his face. Satisfaction threatens to consume me.

"I will *never* kneel before you," I hiss, spittle flying from my mouth. "I will *never* be your perfect daughter. I will *never* be your success story. Want to know why, father?"

His snarl is all the confirmation I need.

"Because I will always be the sinner whose spirit you couldn't crush. Not with your fists and certainly not with your hatred. Hit me if you must. It won't change who I am."

"Please, Ariel," Leah sobs from behind me. "Just stop."

I round on her. "Even now, you won't stand up, will you?"

Thick rivulets of grief course down her cheeks as she glances between me and my father, the terror quaking her limbs.

"I'm not you," she chokes out. "Run if you must. I'm going to stay."

My own tears fall, betrayal and heartbreak warring within me.

"You've corrupted this poor lamb long enough," Pastor Kane booms. "She doesn't want to follow in your unholy footsteps, Ariel. This is your road to travel alone."

"No! I won't let you hurt her. Never."

"She must repent and seek the Lord's heavenly forgiveness." Reaching between his robes, I catch a flash of metal and leather. "It is my responsibility to save those who have lost their way."

Planting my feet, I refuse to move. Even as he draws the belt into his hands. I'll take each strike owed to us twice over if needed. There's already something broken inside of me. I won't allow him to beat and bruise Leah's fragile spirit too.

"Move aside," Pastor Kane demands.

"Never. You taught me to revere God. I'll bow for nobody else."

"I am the Lord's servant, treacherous daughter. You will submit to my will!"

"You speak for nothing holy or right! I won't move!"

"I don't love you," a voice croaks.

The entire scene freezes like a broken record. Invisible fists punch my gut, stealing the air straight from my lungs. Leah steps around me, standing tall for the first time in front of my father. She draws to a halt by his side, looking to him with reverence before meeting my eyes.

"I don't love you," she repeats.

"I don't....I don't understand."

"I think she has made it clear." Pastor Kane drops a meaty palm to her head. "You've led this young girl astray, and she is returning home. You will not continue on this path any longer."

"Leah?" I squeak.

She can barely look at me, blinded by her tears. "You should go."

"Not without you."

"I don't want to see you again, Ariel! Leave!"

Her voice reaches a desperate screech, making my feet move of their own accord. I'm being ripped apart at the seams, splintering into jagged pieces. I can't hold them together without Leah.

"You promised," I accuse. "You said I wouldn't drown."

"Maybe that's what you deserve." Her eyes incline back up to my father, wide and begging. "Please, Pastor Kane. Forgive me. It's my fault, I should be punished. Not Ariel."

There's a heavy thunk as the belt falls from his grasp. Considering her, my father's lips twist in a pleasured smirk. It's the same look he gets before boxing me in, ready to unleash his divine wrath. He's always doled out punishment with the solemn satisfaction of a captain steering his ship.

The worst time was when he made me crawl inside the huge church oven before shutting the door, to illustrate what it would feel like to burn in hell. I emerged relatively unscathed, but my mind rose like a phoenix from the ashes of that dark moment.

"Kneel," he orders again.

I take another step back as Leah's knees hit the floor. The zip of his fly makes me go dizzy. Her eyes squeeze shut as the tears continue to stream. My father palms his erect length, rubbing it from base to tip.

"Prove your loyalty, little lamb. You must earn my forgiveness."

"Don't do it, Leah!" I scream uselessly.

She spares me a bleak glance. "Leave! I don't love you! Go!"

Still stroking himself, my father can't help but leer at me. "If you show yourself here again, I'll kill you. You've brought shame on this church with your sickness."

"Don't worry," I spit out. "I won't be back."

I'm not sure how I move. Some basic kind of survival instinct kicks in, like my mind knows I won't survive watching Leah lose herself so fully. I've seen the other children that earn the pastor's forgiveness with their mouths. They aren't all there anymore. Hollow-eyed and well-trained, reciting the teachings that condone their abuse.

I don't know how, but I run.

Feet thumping and heart exploding.

I run and run and run.

Even as Leah's cries intensify. Even as I'm torn to shreds by the sound of evil unfolding behind me. Even as the world catches alight and burns to the ground without her there to keep me sane. I don't know where I'm running to, nor do I care.

All I know is that I cannot stay—not for him, not for the church, and certainly not for her.

CHAPTER
TWO

LEAH

9 Years Later

PACING THE BUSY CAR PARK, I fist my long hair and tug on the roots. Pain races across my scalp, cutting through the suffocating grasp that anxiety holds on my lungs. I'm going to pass out if I can't get a breath in.

The therapist at the hospital tried to teach me some breathing techniques before I was sent on my way with leaflets and meaningless platitudes. I never paid attention to his ramblings, content to let my mind take me back to a happy place.

Afternoons spent hiding in the corn fields, laughing and joking over stolen wine. She was the only person that could tease such light-hearted happiness out of me after losing my mother.

My blonde-haired devil.

The temptress to my heaven-bound soul.

With shaking hands, I light a cigarette and take the smoke deep into my lungs. I've fallen to my knees, hidden behind a dumpster. As the panic attack passes its peak, I let the curling smoke provide a shallow sense of comfort.

It's a novelty to smoke, despite re-entering society nearly six months ago. Freedom is still a little alien to me. I was overwhelmed by the world and all its endless variety. Heck, I still am. It's all so much.

Once the cigarette is finished, I get my jelly legs beneath me. There's no avoiding it. This support group was part of the deal of my discharge. Apparently, other people who have experienced *religious extremism* gather to talk once a week. I still struggle with that term.

While the past nine years of my life have indeed been extreme, on many levels, it feels normal. They said it would take time for me to accept everything I've seen and being subjected to.

The regular beatings, some performed in front of the entire village. Putting sinners in the middle of a circle and shaming them to the point of devastation—fists and blood and all things evil. Rules and regulations upon our souls, telling us how to live, who to love, when to die.

I can't talk about the other stuff.

Not even to the shrinks.

Ever since Pastor Kane was arrested and St Lucien's was officially disbanded, I've been free falling. I ran hard and fast, never once stopping for a breath. When I do, I remember. And that's when the bad thoughts creep in, like that night when I swallowed all the pills I could find in my ex-roommate's cupboard.

"Come on, Leah," I scold myself. "Walk in there and smile like you mean it."

The support group is being held in a bland, cinderblock building. I'm relieved that it isn't in a church. That would've been the final straw. Keeping my chin tucked low and brown hair loose to hide my face, I sneak inside. There are several people hanging around, male and female alike, but I greet no one.

In the closest chair, I tuck my trembling hands in my coat. I'm wearing plain blue jeans and a loose white t-shirt, nothing fancy. I don't like attention, invisibility keeps me safe. I learned that trick quickly when things got bad in Darkling Heath. Letting others take the abuse instead of me is one of my most shameful regrets.

"Alright everyone, let's take our seats!"

The cheerful voice draws everyone to the circle, the seats slowly filling up. I don't dare look up. Low murmurings and the hair standing up on my neck tell me enough. My presence has been noted.

"Hey there, would you like to introduce yourself? I'm Chelsea."

Terror flares inside of me, hot and sticky like rivulets of blood.

"It's Leah." I stare at my feet.

"Welcome to the group, Leah. We're glad to have you."

The chatter fades into an insignificant hum, washing over my head. I stare down at my second-hand trainers, given to me by the hospital when I was discharged to wear home. A little fish thrown back into a big pond, terrified, but determined to drown. I don't want to be here.

Nobody tries to talk to me again. They must sense my hostility a mile off. I'm not a rude person, more like too exhausted to exist. I only register the bang of the door being thrown open when hurried footsteps interrupt the meeting.

"Wait, I'm here!"

Oh, hell no.

This can't be happening.

I feel like I've been defibrillated and knocked unconscious all at once, the shock and excitement mixing into a blur. Despite everything, I still believe that God has a plan. I should've known I would find her again.

"You're late," Chelsea scolds.

"I got stuck with a client, I apologise."

Like a puppet on a string, my eyes are lifted up for the first time. Dancing over countless bored and medicated faces, warily watching each other for an impending break down. Chelsea, a middle-aged woman with warmth in her eyes, looks mildly annoyed at the intrusion.

Fate guides my gaze further afield. Up and up, dragging my damaged soul back home. She's stalking towards the circle, a sophisticated cream coat tucked under one arm, and an expensive purse and phone clutched in her ring-laden hand. I don't recognise the person attached to that raspy voice.

Her once blonde hair is now a vibrant shade of cotton candy pink, barely brushing her razor sharp jawline. The dark swirls of floral tattoos cover her entire arm from shoulder to wrist, matching multiple rows of piercings in her ears and another in her nose. Her eyes are stained bright violet by artificial contacts, completely changing her identity.

The entire room falls away.

Nothing exists but the rise and fall of her chest.

The pitiful distance between us.

All the years of history keeping us apart.

Ariel doesn't spot me at first, her laser focus set on the single empty chair. Her supple, curvaceous body is highlighted by skin-tight leather jeans and a low cut blouse, paired off with towering high heels. She's exposing skin that would be severely punished back home. Her cleavage is almost entirely on show, and I fight the urge to shout.

Sinner.

Whore.

Demon.

"Stop it," I mutter to myself. "He isn't here."

I'm wrong. Pastor Kane is always here, no matter how far I run. He lives in the shadowy corners of my mind, the violent depths of my nightmares, and the lonely interludes of my life.

"Leah, allow me to introduce our latecomer," Chelsea says. "This is Ariel."

Her words drop like a sledgehammer. I take my last shred of

courage and lift my gaze. Out of 65 million people on this godforsaken island, I had to find her. I've prayed for it. Begged for another chance. Pleaded with the world to give me a break.

I never expected it to happen.

Sinners like me don't deserve such luck.

I'm standing before I realise, trembling like a leaf and sweating buckets. Neither of us moves. Nobody else speaks. We're facing off on two sides of a bottomless chasm. One step closer to the other, and both of us will plummet to our deaths.

"Wildflower," Ariel whispers in disbelief.

The nickname slashes me like a knife to the throat. I stumble through the circle without breathing, accidentally shoving someone from their seat in my haste to escape. Ariel tries to grab me as I run past, shouting my name again.

I don't stop.

Not until I'm outside and fresh air is battling to enter my constricted lungs. With gravel digging into my hands, I let my forehead meet the ground. I'm shaking too much to stand up. I don't bother running further, I know she'll find me.

Ariel is nothing if not loyal, and fiercely so. It used to be one of her best qualities. She loves with every single fibre of her being. It killed me to hurt her so badly that she had no choice but to leave me behind. It was the only way to keep her safe.

"Leah?" she asks uncertainly.

"It's me," I choke out.

"I don't know what to say. You're here."

Feeling my cheeks sting with tears, I surprise myself by struggling to my feet. Everything is swaying and ticking like a lucid dream. This doesn't feel real. But she's there, inches away, staring at me like I'm the best thing she's ever seen. I can almost see the face of the girl I once knew.

"You're here," she repeats in a daze.

"Looks like it. Hi."

"Can I…hug you?"

Shaking my hands out, I nod. "Yeah s-sure."

Before I know it, I'm crushed against Ariel's chest. Her arms band around me, cutting off my blood supply. Her breath stirs my hair, fingers digging deep into my back, heart hammering against my skin.

All proof that this is real.

I'm not dreaming.

Then the moment breaks. Ariel shoves me away, accusation and rage painted across her unfamiliar face. Feeling like my skin is melting from my bones, I hug my midsection, ready to take the inevitable punishment.

"What are you doing here? Did you track me down?"

"N-No...I w-wasn't looking for you," I stutter.

Her scoff is bitter. "I guessed as much. You made it very clear how you felt nine years ago."

My head shakes robotically. "No."

"You told me to leave because you didn't love me, if I recall. Though you loved sucking my father's cock, right? You didn't even put up a fight before bowing to him."

"No—"

"I don't know if I even want to see you. Fuck, Leah. Nine years! You rock up after nine goddamn years and look at me like I just kicked your fucking puppy. What the hell?"

"No," I repeat, unable to muster another word.

"No what?" Ariel grabs me by the shoulders and shakes me. "No fucking what? I loved you, dammit! I loved you and I walked away. Just like you told me to."

More tears race down my cheeks. "Please stop..."

"Look at you! What happened?"

"Stop!" I scare Ariel enough to make her jump.

She stumbles back when I shove her. There's an inferno raging inside of me, threatening to drag me to the burning depths of hell where sinners like me belong. When I shove Ariel again, she snaps and pushes me back.

We end up wrestling, both vying to punch the other, screaming with ceaseless fury. The metallic clatter of something hitting the ground cuts through the haze. Ariel's eyes dart up and down several times, looking from me to the gun now laying between us.

Fire burns across my cheeks.

I'm ashamed by the weakness it reveals.

Clutching her tightly, I need to hold on for balance. Her anger has melted into shock, concern and fear. I've never seen Ariel look afraid. She's always been the strong one, larger than life, determined to enjoy every last breath on this earth.

"Why are you carrying a gun?" she demands.

With an elbow jabbed into her ribs, I scoop up the weapon and tuck it back inside my coat. Ariel stands there, watching my every move, but I refuse to meet her eyes again.

"I have to go," I mutter. "Goodbye, Ariel."

This time, she grabs me.

"Don't walk away, Leah."

"You don't need me here."

A frustrated breath whooshes from her lungs. "Just give me half an hour. That's all I want. Half an hour and if you still want to leave, you can. We can't leave things like this."

The gun burns a hole in my pocket as I consider her offer. You can buy anything out here if you know the right people. I'm not the timid, scared child that ran from Pastor Kane and his fists. With enough determination, you can do whatever you want.

I bought the illegal gun for a reason.

I intend to fulfil the promise that I made to myself.

No more.

"Please, wildflower."

"Don't call me that," I snarl.

Ariel runs a hand over her lurid pink hair, tousling the short, immaculately styled length. Even her expressions are different, older and wiser. Desire and infatuation have melted into resignation and defeat. We're not the people we used to be.

Nothing will ever bring those two innocent girls back to

themselves. But perhaps, I owe her this much. A single conversation.

Maybe that's why I've failed in my quest to end my life until now. God isn't done with me yet. I have one last door to close that has been trapped open and gushing grief for so many years.

I broke her heart.

She left me to die.

Neither of us deserves this life, but I'll take the fall for our sins. I owe her that much. She can live on, while I burn for an eternity in hell.

"Half an hour."

Her eyes snap up to mine. "Really?"

"I owe you that much. After that, I'll leave you in peace."

"You think I've had a second of peace after leaving you?" Ariel offers tonelessly. "Living and surviving are two very different things. You of all people should know that. Come on, I know where we can go."

Despite everything, she offers me her hand. I stare at it warily, noting the silver rings and signs of wealth. She's like the snake in the Garden of Eden, tempting Eve to her downfall. Only there's no apple for me to bite, I've already lost my soul long ago. There's no saving me now.

"You can keep the gun," she adds in a low voice. "For now."

Defeat settles over me like an ash cloud as I nod.

"Lead the way."

CHAPTER
THREE

ARIEL

THE SUN SINKS low on the horizon, brilliant beams of burnt orange and pink painting the ocean waves. Wide cliffs surround the secluded beach, protecting the bay from wind and onlookers.

It feels like we're Martians exploring a foreign land, devoid of any other human life. I chose this remote seaside town for its privacy. In the off season, nobody comes here. It's a life trapped in stasis for those glorious few months.

I spend my days in solitude and nights in sin. The nearby city provides the perfect clientele for my work. Being able to step away from that and walk beside the ocean waves allows me to escape reality when needed.

"Here, give me your hand."

Leah eyes me with trepidation, her brown hair cascading down her back. I always thought her lake water eyes looked haunted, but the light that once burned within them has truly been extinguished. She barely looks like the memory I've spent night after night recalling.

"It's steep." I indicate to the craggy rocks.

Tentatively taking my hand, I help her hop down the remaining steps. Pausing to pull off my favourite heels, I let my toes sink into the wet sand. I don't care that it's freezing cold.

I've discovered that life consists of snapshots, glimpses of freedom, moments of joy amidst the darkness. I grab hold of those moments with both hands at every opportunity. Fuck the cold.

"This is beautiful," she says quietly.

"I like to come here and think. It's always deserted."

"Sounds peaceful."

"The rest of my life isn't."

Together, we walk across the abandoned beach. Fading sunlight warms our skin, the ethereal, golden glow seeming to encapsulate the angel by my side. She looks heavenly, even in her too-thin, washed out state. I can barely tear my eyes away from her.

"How long have you been in town?" I ask carefully.

Leah shrugs. "Only a week or two, I move around a lot."

"Where were you before?"

A shutter falls over her. "Hospital."

"Are you sick?"

"Probably."

I release a breath. "Sick with what?"

Leah manages a thin smile. "Incurable sadness."

Sensing the storm brewing between us, I bite my lip to hold back the barrage of questions. I'm on very thin ice here. The last thing I want is to scare her away again. I'm a master of playing the game and manipulating information out of people.

All my clients like to do is talk about themselves. Even while trussed up and utterly at my mercy, the secrets spill from their lips easier than breathing. The more they talk, the more money I add to the clock. Only when they have bared their souls do I begin the sweet torture.

"How long have you been...out?"

Her dull eyes flick to mine. "St Lucien's was disbanded six months ago after a criminal investigation. I've been bouncing around since."

"Alone? What about your pops?"

"I'll see him at the trial," she murmurs. "The prosecution wants me to testify."

Her revelation drops like a lead weight. Shaking off my hand, she walks alone to the water's edge. Her pale feet dip into the waves as her eyes slide shut. I stand back slightly, content to worship at her altar, still thunderstruck that she's here.

"How do you do it?" Leah asks.

Regardless of my designer leather jeans, I join her in the ice cold water. The sun has almost disappeared, cloaking the world in that strange period of twilight. Caught between light and dark, life and death. A land for lost things and broken reunions.

"Do what, wildflower?"

Her fingers seek out mine, tangling together. "Live."

I tuck my arm around Leah's narrow waist. The scent of cheap shampoo tickles my nose from her impossibly long hair. I'm sure she was forbidden from cutting it back in Darkling Heath. I let my impulsive cut grow out, but still keep it short as my own act of defiance.

"Living is the easy part," I answer. "You breathe, blink, eat and drink. It's living with yourself that's the challenge. Living with the person you've become."

"You're here, aren't you? After everything…everything…*he* did."

My teeth bite into my lip. "Pastor Kane?"

Leah's eyes empty of all recognition as she stares at the horizon, dark clouds of night swarming ever closer. I hold her tighter, but it feels like I'm clinging to a fading ghost.

"My father, too."

I digest that, violence thrumming down my spine. "You were there for all these years? Why didn't you run when things got bad?"

"Sometimes the unknown is scarier than the pain. I'm used to hurting. Without it, I'm not sure who I am. Hurting myself is the only thing that makes sense to me now."

The beginnings of an idea steal my attention. What Leah

doesn't know is that I make my living off inflicting pain. Trauma is an untameable beast. It isn't fixed with textbook advice and expensive therapy. Control must be retaken, one memory at a time.

"I own a business now," I begin, drawing her attention. "I struggled at first, after I left. I'd always been taught that my wants and desires were wrong, sinful, disgusting. It took a long time to unpick those threads."

"What kind of business?" Leah frowns.

Here goes nothing.

"I'm what you would call a dominatrix."

The roar of crashing waves falls into the background as we stare into each other's eyes. I can see the questions and confusion brimming in her foggy irises, but Leah doesn't let go of my hand. Not yet.

"I take on clients who agree to surrender their control to me," I continue. "It's always consensual and pleasurable. We explore different things they may like."

"What kind of clients?"

"Lots of the people I see are healing from some pretty fucked-up stuff. I give them the space to rediscover their sexuality, take back their lives."

"And it works?"

Halting, I force Leah to look at me. "Depends how ready you are to move on with your life. I can't help someone that's already given up. You have to want it. This isn't any normal kind of therapy."

She surrenders her abused lip. "I don't know what I want."

Easing my hand inside her coat, I find the gun and pull it out. Leah swallows hard, looking anywhere but at me or the offending item. I'm familiar with the model, it's a cheap make that you can easily find on a shady street corner. With my finger on the trigger, I press the barrel to her temple.

Leah's eyes blow wide, shifting between desperation and terror. I can read the truth from her. She wants me to pull the trigger and take the choice away, end the eternal push and pull with that dark voice in her mind. I click the safety off and watch her gulp again.

"Bang," I whisper. "Now you're dead. Is that what you want?"

"Maybe."

"And how do you feel right now, with me holding this gun to your head? Knowing that I could end your life in a split second with no one here to see? Hell, I doubt anybody would even notice your absence."

I can see the fire inside of her reacting to my insult. Just a glimmer. A tantalising flash. In this brief moment, there's a glimpse of life in her long-dead shell. Enough for me to grab hold of.

There's my girl.

"It feels like living," she replies.

Satisfied, I lower the gun. "That's control. I don't make love to my clients. I hurt them, bruise them, break them. Whatever it takes to reignite that spark. You can't survive without hurting. Well, neither can I."

There's a beat of silence, then her plea comes.

"What if I need you to hurt me?"

Looking back down at the gun, I test its weight. All while Leah watches, her feet shifting anxiously. I'm sure my father's voice is echoing in her head at this very moment, because I certainly know he is in mine.

I'm everything Pastor Kane hates in this world.

Sin. Pleasure.

Desire. Empowerment.

I'm going to fix the damage he has caused us both.

"You'll need to sign a contract."

Leah nods so hard, I fear her neck will break.

"I don't...uh, have any money."

"I don't want your money," I fire back. "If we do this, you have to promise me one night. Just one more night, alright?"

"One night?"

Aiming the gun at myself, I love the thrilling weight of it in my hands. "One night before you pull this trigger." I mime blowing my brains out. "That's what you're carrying it around for, right? To fire it?"

Leah doesn't answer, but also doesn't deny it. I know it's the truth without her meaningless words. I can see the hopelessness cemented inside of her like a cancer, slowly corroding her from within. I've felt similarly over the years when the nights seemed endless and the world too much to bear.

"You give me one night to show you that living with all we've been through is possible," I state plainly. "If by the end of our night, you want to pull that trigger, I won't stop you. You're free to carry on."

"You would let me walk away?"

"You let me do exactly that, didn't you?"

She visibly gulps. "I thought I was protecting you."

Clicking the safety back on the gun, I tuck it in the pocket of my coat. "Yeah, well this is me protecting you. I'll give you this back after. Then your life is in your hands again."

Turning on my heel, I march back up the sand bank. Darkness has fully invaded the beach now, leaving us stranded in the night. The crash of waves re-enters my awareness as I move further away. When I'm around Leah, it's like the entire world ceases to exist.

That terrifies and exhilarates me.

"Ariel?"

I glance back to find her rooted to the spot. "Yeah?"

Leah shuffles her feet again, the panic etched across every inch of her frame. The urge to gather her in my arms, wrap her in cotton wool and hide her from the entire world nearly bowls me over.

I can't do that.

Not anymore.

She needs to feel again.

I will have to hurt her to prove a point. This bullshit life, it's worth living. Even if it hurts like hell. She can take that pain and fashion it into armour, use it to steel herself against the world. All I need to do is show her the way.

"I didn't mean what I said," she says awkwardly. "I just wanted to get you as far away from that place as possible. Even if it meant throwing away everything we had. I was willing to pay that price."

"You should've run with me," I interrupt. "Now we're both too broken for this world and left to scavenge for the pieces left behind. You have a chance. Don't waste it again."

I leave her standing on the beach, entirely alone.

Without looking back, I know she will follow me.

CHAPTER
FOUR

LEAH

SITTING in the back of the taxicab, my leg shakes uncontrollably beneath my long trench coat. My skin is covered in gooseflesh, fully on display in the skimpy outfit Ariel had delivered to my one-room bedsit. The note was brief and straight to the point.

Wear this.

One night.

Always yours, A x

With her work address rattled off to the driver, I settled back for the ride into the nearest city. It took over an hour with my nose pressed against the glass, taking in the dizzying heights of skyscrapers and endless gleaming lights.

The closer we draw to her address, the harder my heart pounds. I have no idea what to expect from tonight. Perhaps, a glimmer of hope.

Maybe even salvation.

God put her on my path for a reason.

The taxi parks in a swanky, downtown suburb draped in metropolitan glamour. Tall, three storey townhouses carved from stone and wide marble steps box me in. Windows reveal their secrets in the late night haze.

Families are sitting down to eat, while husbands shout at wives. Children kiss their parents goodnight, and old married couples reminisce about the past. The untameable dance of life plays out in real time.

One house stands darkened with the thick velvet curtains drawn. I can see the number laid out in shining brass upon the black lacquered door. Passing off the last of my remaining cash, I step out into the chilly night, throwing my single bag of possessions over my shoulder.

There's no going back now. I can't afford the trip home and I packed up my meagre belongings in ten minutes flat. No matter what happens, I won't be returning to the bedsit. Hell, I won't be returning anywhere.

Tonight is do or die.

Time to put my faith in something again.

My bare legs peek out from beneath my coat as I climb the steps. Listening to the chime of the doorbell only heightens my anxiety. I'm ashamed to admit it, but I'm already slick between my thighs. The sheer anticipation of the unknown has rekindled something in me I long thought dead.

When Ariel swings the door open, my breath catches. Reconciling this woman with the reckless, adorable child I once knew is dizzying. Wrapped in a blood-red silk robe, flashing suspenders and stockings that match her spotless heels, Ariel is every inch the devil in disguise.

Her candy floss hair has been lightly tousled, paired with flawless smokey makeup and dark, dramatic lips. Black painted nails tap against the door as Ariel sizes me up, from the borrowed coat to the small bag over my shoulder. The slightest smile tugs her glossed lips.

"You came."

I shift on my feet. "You didn't think I would?"

"I hoped. Seemed safer to prepare for disappointment."

Gesturing with a wide sweep of her arm, I take a final breath and step into the lion's den. The door slams behind me with a solemn proclamation. I take in the grand hallway lit with crystal chandeliers and full-height gilded mirrors.

"How does a teen runaway afford this place?" I ask warily.

Ariel takes my bag without asking, hanging it on a coat hook. "I've been doing my job for a long time. This kind of work pays well to say the least. Not many would admit it, but everyone needs a place to surrender themselves."

"And that's what they do? Surrender to you?"

Taking the lead, she begins to ascend the spiral staircase leading into the unknown. I tighten my trench coat around me and follow her, feeling like my heart will tear from my chest at any moment.

"There's power in surrendering," she explains, heading for a closed door. "Only those who are free can choose to put their life in the hands of another. What could be more powerful than that?"

Allowing me to pass, I'm guided into a shadowy office. Walls built from glossy shelves and framed pieces of art meet dark floorboards covered in Persian rugs. Ariel props a hip on the corner of the huge desk, shuffling through pre-prepared paperwork as I hover.

"You seem to have it all figured out." I rub the back of my neck. "I don't understand why you were at that support group. Why bother going at all?"

Without breaking eye contact, she offers me a manilla folder. "Even I have to recharge when things get tough, seek support in others. It's what keeps me going, remembering where I've been, and where I'm going."

Peering inside the folder, I find a stack of papers. A quick scan over the contents is enough to chill my blood. It's a fairly detailed contract, denoting many clauses. The legal jargon makes my brain hurt.

"Should I read all of this?" I sigh.

"If you don't trust me, then yes."

"And if I do trust you? Is that enough?"

Ariel reaches out, her thumb skating over my cheek. A shiver travels down my spine, the furnace inside of me being stoked higher with a single touch. I remember the way she used to kiss me.

Taste me.

Toy with me.

I've only pleasured myself since, more often than not to her memory. Trusting anyone else with the physical act of love was an impossibility. The only person I want to touch me is standing in this room.

"I will keep you safe," Ariel murmurs. "If you want to stop, you will say the safe word *indigo*. I'm going to push you, challenge you. It won't be easy going. You're fighting for your life, aren't you?"

There's no sense in lying.

"I have no plans to continue like this," I admit lowly.

Her thumb runs over my bottom lip next, briefly dipping inside my mouth. I surprise myself by accepting the digit, letting my tongue swirl over the tip without being told. I can see the command in her violet eyes.

"Then tonight is the battle of your life," she whispers. "Are you ready to follow me into the dark? Will you surrender yourself to me completely, and trust that I'll show you the light again?"

My knees knock together as I answer. "Yes. Please help me."

I sign on the dotted line and hand back the folder, my nerves fading into excitement. With a nod, Ariel takes my hand. I'm led from the office, back down the hallway to a final door. Ariel unlocks it with a small key before discarding her silk robe on the threshold.

My mouth dries up as I take her in. The dangerously short, PVC dress clings to her like a second skin, laced up over her breasts that are threatening to spill out. With her long legs wrapped in stockings and even more tattoos than I noticed before, she looks every inch the sinful goddess I know her to be.

Her heels add several inches to her height, making her seem impossibly powerful as she looms over me. The final touch is added with a supple leather mask that Ariel slips over her face, highlighting the vibrant hue of her contact lenses. There are even two inch bunny ears sticking upwards.

Ariel smirks. "Your mouth is hanging open."

"Uh, you look...different. Good."

"It's *you look good, mistress,*" she corrects. "You will always refer to me as that here."

Sticking her hand out, she gestures for me to remove the coat. I'm terrified of the revealing outfit delivered for me to wear, but I'm even more scared of what happens if I leave here empty handed. Seizing that spark of courage, I slowly unfasten the coat and ease it off my shoulders.

"You also look different," Ariel compliments. "It suits you."

Brushing my long hair aside, I glance down at my matching black lingerie. Encasing my small breasts and soaked pussy in lace, the outfit is completed by a thick, leather harness. The straps cut across my chest and stomach, wrapping around my whole body.

I should be running for my life.

Everything about this is totally wrong.

But fuck, I've never felt so damn powerful.

Ariel offers me a hand. "Come along, my fallen angel. Tonight, we dine in hell."

Inside the room, soft light gives way to rich brocade paper and blacked out windows. The room is dominated by a huge, four poster bed, covered in bright purple silk sheets. I spot the gold hooks and bolt holes built in, presumably to tie someone up. I've watched lots of porn in the last six months to satisfy my curiosity. This is the real deal.

On the other side of the room, a massive dresser fills the space. All manner of items are there on display, most made from leather or metal, endless sharp points and soft, buttery straps. I can recognise a few from my research. Floggers. Whips.

Spankers. Gags. Jesus Christ, are those clamps? I'm blushing before I know it.

"Last chance to walk away," Ariel warns.

Instead, I approach the bed and stop at the end. I don't look at her as I fall to my knees, like I did for her father so many times, only this time it isn't out of fear. I can barely think through the adrenaline riding me so hard, my clit is practically pulsing.

"No, mistress," I whisper.

The click of the door closing almost makes me jump. Her heels mark her approach, then light fingertips graze over my hair. I shudder as she gently plaits the long length, tying it off with a rubber band. Letting my eyes slide shut, I focus on nothing but her fragrant, honeysuckle scent.

"On the bed," she murmurs.

"Yes, mistress."

With numb legs, I climb on the bed. Ariel watches as I slide down the silk sheets, spreading my shaking body out. Seemingly satisfied, she stops at the dresser to gather her supplies. My stomach flips at the length of thick rope tucked under her arm when she returns.

"Hands above your head, legs spread apart."

I hesitate, suddenly nervous again.

Ariel's gaze darkens and she uses the end of the rope to strike me. It whips against my bare leg, sending pain shooting up my spine. I stare at the rising red welt, hit by a wave of satisfaction.

"If you want me to hurt you again, you'll do as you're told," she orders.

I do want that.

More than anything.

I can actually feel my dead heart *beating* again.

"Sorry, mistress."

Spread-eagled like Christ on the crucifix, Ariel sets to work restraining me to the bed. The rope burns my wrists and ankles as I'm tied up, the material pulled taut to allow me no room to escape. Once done, she surveys my body with satisfaction.

"I can't tell you how many times I imagined having you here," she admits. "I dreamed of punishing you for breaking my heart. Now that I'm here, I realise I would've done the same if it got you out."

She trails a fingernail along my collar bone, dragging down the straps of the harness and reaching my lower belly. My hips try to shift on instinct, begging for more. Ariel tuts under her breath, teasing the very edge of my lace panties.

When she ducks her head down to see my body better, a blush takes over me. I was unnerved by the crotchless design when I first unwrapped the lingerie but now, I feel so damn sexy. She stares at my cunt with heat burning in her eyes, those red painted lips slightly parted.

"Perfect little angel. Stay right there for me."

I watch her PVC-covered ass sashay across the room. Ariel studies the various toys and instruments on display, selecting a leather riding crop and a long, black dildo. I've seen girls fucking each other with them online. In St Lucien's, we only had our fingers and tongues.

"Are you going to put that in me?" I ask curiously.

Tossing the dildo on the bed sheets, Ariel flexes the riding crop in her hands. I cry out when she hits my bare belly with it first, before dragging it upwards to tease my stiffened nipples through the lace bra.

"Did I say you could speak?"

I bite my tongue to hold back a response.

"Better," she praises.

Tingles race over me as Ariel teases me with the smooth leather, circling my sensitised flesh. When she runs it over my mouth, encouraging me to open up, I flick my tongue out to wet the riding crop. Nodding her approval, Ariel moves it down south and smacks my exposed pussy lips.

I scream out, warmth flooding through my pores. She hits me again between the legs—harder this time. Pain and pleasure become one.

"Scream louder, little bitch," Ariel instructs. "Tell me how much you want it."

"Please," I whimper, my body quaking with need. "Touch me. Hurt me. Do anything."

"There's a good girl. So obedient."

I pull on the restraints as she drags the riding crop up and down my pussy, teasing my aching clit. When she brings it to her own lips and licks my juices from the wet leather, I nearly see stars.

"You still taste the same, wildflower. So goddamn sweet."

Abandoning the riding crop, Ariel picks up the dildo and begins to smother it in lubricant from the bedside table. My mouth goes dry as I watch, staring at the length with fear. Is it going to hurt? I trust her, but I literally have no power here. I can't run, even if I wanted to.

When she runs the tip over my entrance, gently easing it inside of me, I can't suppress a garbled moan. The dildo stretches my pussy with each inch, heightened by the coldness of the lube. I can feel Ariel's attention so acutely as she studies every last reaction on my face.

"Easy now," she instructs. "Don't fight it."

She begins to move the toy. It glides in and out of me, guided by her expert hand, overwhelming me with this feeling I've never experienced before. An odd sense of fullness, with fire racing through my veins and warmth running down my thighs as my release builds.

I yank on the rope holding me prone again, hissing as it burns my wrists. My body wants to buck and writhe, but I can't move an inch. Not even to press my thighs together as the feeling spirals higher. I've made myself come a couple of times, but nothing I did felt like this.

"You want to squirt all over my hand?" Ariel goads.

"Oh God. Yes, I do."

"That name isn't allowed in here!"

Then the pressure between my thighs is gone, ripped away

by her cruelness. I cry out again, mourning the orgasm stolen from my grasp. Ariel stands there smirking like a maniac, holding the glistening dildo, denying me the one thing I want most in the world.

"You don't pray to God here," she informs me. "Pray to me."

"Please, mistress. I want to come."

The glint of malice in her eyes reminds me so much of her father, I can't help but cringe. Ariel spots the reaction a mile off, but rather than seem contrite, her grin widens.

"You have to earn the right to orgasm in this room. You will finish when I say so and not a second sooner."

"Please," I beg again.

"Shut the fuck up, you pious whore. You fall to your knees for my father, but not for me? How is that fair?"

"No...I didn't...I..."

Picking the crop back up, Ariel slaps both of my breasts with it. The zip of pain feels like fireworks are exploding beneath my skin, my nipples pebbling to the point of agony.

"Apologise. I want to hear you grovel," she demands.

Dammit, this is so humiliating.

Why am I so turned on right now?

"I'm so sorry, mistress," I mumble. "It's all my fault."

"I can't hear you."

"I'm sorry! Is that what you want to hear? I hate myself and everything I did to survive." Tears race down my cheeks, mixing grief with overwhelming desire. "I hate that in this moment, I feel more alive than I have in years."

"Because?" Ariel prompts.

I search for the answer as she reaches back into her bedside table, searching for something. When she pulls a black-handled, wickedly sharp knife out, I forget how to breathe entirely.

"Answer me, Leah. Or I won't let you come."

Looming over me, Ariel begins to slowly trail the blade up my left leg. It digs in slightly, leaving a burning sensation. Pleasure and pain collide within me, my pussy aching to be filled again. She will only relieve me when I've admitted all my secrets.

"You know what? Fuck you," I grind out.

"Excuse me?"

"I won't say it."

I gasp as she presses the blade deep into my inner thigh, the warmth of blood spilling down my leg. Gritting my teeth, I bite back a moan of pleasure when she circles her finger in the sticky mess, dragging fresh blood over my clit. Her fingers are like magic, coaxing my compliance.

"You will say it," Ariel commands.

"Go to hell."

Her fingers suddenly push inside me, lubricated with my blood. I can't hold back a cry of pleasure as she begins to fiercely pump them in and out. The building wave begins to rise again, faster this time. I'm desperate for relief.

"Already been there," she says roughly. "We both have. Difference is, I refuse to let the past break me. You're weak. Worthless. Broken. Giving up so easily."

Every inch of me feels like it's been dipped in fire. With sweat beading on my forehead, I pant and prepare to lose myself to the abyss. My orgasm is so close, almost within touching distance. As I ready to give in, Ariel's fingers are ripped away all over again.

"Fuck!" I shout.

"Lying sluts don't get to come. I want the truth, then you can come all over my hand."

Anger rushes over me. I'm used to being numb, detached, locked in the safety of loneliness. The rage feels so alien to me, I can barely control it. I kick and scream, yanking on the restraints until I can feel blood welling up.

Ariel watches, the corner of her mouth tilted up.

"Let me out! We're done. I want to go home."

"No," she says simply.

"What do you mean no?! Indigo!"

Ariel grins. "You signed your life over to me in that contract. Fuck your safe word. I'm doing what has to be done."

My head snaps to the side as she slaps me. It shocks the words right out of my mouth. With my cheek burning and eyes welling up, I stare at her with betrayal. The world almost looks red, I'm so angry.

"What the hell is wrong with you?" I hiss.

"You have to break before you can put yourself back together."

"You're a crazy fucking bitch!"

"And you're a pathetic waste of space. Is that what you want to hear? You want me to confirm all these ridiculous beliefs you have about yourself? Give you a good reason to pull that trigger?"

"Yes! Give me a reason!"

The words slip out without my permission. If I could, I'd slap my hand over my mouth. The satisfaction is written all across Ariel's sadistic expression. She picks the dildo back up, this time lubricating it with the blood still flowing from my injured leg.

"Stop," I plead.

Ariel doesn't listen, pushing it back inside of me. I can't stop her from violating me while my legs are pinned wide open. She pushes the toy in so deep, I feel like I'm going to implode. The indecision only makes my arousal more intense as my mind and body battle one another.

"I won't give you a reason," she states calmly. "You don't deserve it. If you pull that trigger, you do it for yourself. I want to see you live. Heal. Grow. I won't visit your fucking grave, Leah. No way."

I'm sobbing and moaning at the same time, too confused to throw any more insults at her. When the promise of an orgasm hits me for a third time, Ariel doesn't withhold it. My entire body is wracked by sensation, so intense my vision dims. I scream out her name, a prayer and condemnation all in one.

"That's my perfect girl," she croons.

Still riding the waves of my climax, I'm unprepared for her hands wrapping around my throat. A squeak escapes my lips as Ariel straddles my chest, her dress riding so high on her hips, I catch a flash of her bare pussy. She presses a kiss to my forehead before beginning to squeeze.

"I said I'd take you to your breaking point. I hope you still trust me, wildflower, because I'm going to hurt you now. I'm going to make you see the light."

More tears pour from my eyes as her grip tightens even more. I cannot breathe at all. My lungs are on fire, begging for air that's being stolen away. Pulling on the tightly knotted rope, I battle to escape her wrath, but the demon sitting on my chest doesn't relent. She bares her teeth as she squeezes the life from me.

I'm going to die.

Ariel doesn't want to fix me.

She's going to kill me.

The room dims again, beginning to go fuzzy at the edges. Moving one hand down my body while keeping the other at my throat, Ariel finds my dripping pussy. I'm still wet, despite the brutal torture of her touch.

Her fingers easily glide inside of me. After a few pumps, she pushes one against the tight muscle of my asshole. I try to cry out at the intrusion, but I can't say a single thing.

I'm going to pass out if she doesn't relent. Ariel begins to finger fuck me in both holes, still dominating my airway, and that's when I see it. A glimmering mirage in the vast expanse of the desert.

The light.

It's there, over her shoulder.

"I'm taking you right to the edge," she whispers in my ear. "You don't have my permission to die. Not now, not ever. I won't watch you kill yourself for that man. He doesn't deserve it."

My eyelids start to droop, too heavy to hold up. The light is growing stronger, burning my retinas with its intensity. Ariel curls a finger deep in my pussy at that exact moment, triggering another implosion. I'm dying and climaxing at the same time. It's fucking terrifying, no longer being in control of my fate.

"Look at that light," Ariel instructs in a low, sultry purr. "Take a long, hard look. It's time to say goodbye, Leah. Say goodbye to the person you are. Throw her into the flames. She doesn't get to define your future."

At the very last second, her punishing clamp on my airway releases. I cough and splutter, the air offending my lungs that have long since given up hope of breathing again. Ariel still straddles me as I sob, blinded by an invisible light that only I can see.

I want it to take me.

Embrace me.

Free me.

But as the light recedes, the dark tether pulling me into the grave snaps. I watch the world settle back around me with an overwhelming sense of ecstasy, her touch dragging the release from my imprisoned body. I feel so much all at once, hit by wave after wave of emotion.

Pain. Pleasure.

Grief. Despair.

Desire. Love.

Hatred.

"Let yourself feel, my beautiful wildflower," Ariel coaxes. "You've been numb for too long. You don't have to just survive anymore. You're free. It's time to live."

Her lips smash against mine in a fierce kiss, reclaiming the slivers of glorious air I've been so generously afforded. Our tongues fight and dance, two deadly warriors determined to possess the other.

She tastes like death and destruction. Hope and salvation. Freedom and imprisonment. Everything I've wanted since I woke up in that hospital and all I've been running from.

A lifeline.

A reason to go on.

When the kiss breaks, the click of a gun causes my eyes to fling open. Ariel is staring down at me with complete calmness, holding my gun to her own temple. The safety is clicked off as her finger dances on the trigger. I scream her name, begging the ropes that are holding me to break.

"Ariel! Stop!"

I'm offered a bright, powerful smile. It feels like the sun is shining down on me as I rise from the icy depths of the Antarctic Ocean, glimpsing the light for the first time in years. She's shown me a sliver of what could be. My heart already wants more of this feeling.

"Ariel!" I scream again.

My entire world ends when she pulls the trigger.

CHAPTER FIVE
ARIEL

THE CLICK of the empty chamber rings out like a gunshot. I might as well have set off a nuclear bomb in the darkened bedroom.

In Leah's eyes, once empty even the tiniest hint of recognition, too many emotions to label war for supremacy. She looks so terrified, like she's hanging on the edge of oblivion, screaming for someone to pull her back up to safety.

The gun is empty.

Nothing fired.

Releasing the trigger, I cock the gun, urging her mind to catch up. Shock hits her first. More tears. Gasping breaths. Panic and fear constricting her lungs better than I ever could. When she realises it was a bluff, the anger returns.

Sweet, beautiful rage.

Hello again, old friend.

"How could you," she accuses through her tears.

"I'm sorry, Leah."

"I thought…I thought…"

"That I was going to die?"

"Yes! Fuck…I can't breathe."

Lowering the gun, I use my spare hand to cup her soaked

cheek. She's trembling all over, her entire body struggling to make sense of what I've just put her through. I swipe her tears aside with my thumb, content to die if it means I can stare at her forever.

"Now you know how it would feel," I whisper gently. "I know it hurts. The pain washes over you, over and over, refusing to abate even as you choke and drown. That's how trauma feels."

"It never stops," she hiccups

Leah's cries only increase. Retrieving my knife, I slash through the rope holding her arms. Her wrists are weeping blood from how hard she's struggled. Once free, she immediately seeks me out.

Frantic fingers rip the leather mask from my face. Leah angrily tosses it to the floor, then strokes my cheek, my jaw, everywhere. Searching for proof that the gun was indeed empty.

"You can choose to swim with the current," I continue softly. "You don't have to battle against it any longer. The life raft is in sight. It's coming. You don't have to be alone anymore."

"I thought...I thought I lost you."

"I will follow you to the ends of this cruel world, wildflower. I'll do whatever it takes to keep you in this life. You're not allowed to walk into the light yet."

With all the restraints cut away, she's free at last. I expect her to run and curl up in the furthest corner of the room. I've had intense sessions before, but this was on another level.

I watch Leah blink and look down at her free limbs, verifying that it's over. Gingerly sitting up, one hand stroking the rapidly forming bruises on her throat, she looks ready to bolt. I wouldn't blame her after that.

I'm surprised instead when her arms wrap around me. Trapped against her chest, I listen to the pounding of her heart. She sounds like she's having a heart attack, but she doesn't let go.

"I'm not alone," Leah chants. "I'm not alone."

"You're not alone," I say back. "I've been drowning in those waves for a very long time. Some days, I don't come up for air. I want to be your life raft, Leah. And I want you to be mine."

Disentangling myself from her embrace, I slip my hand under the silk pillow beneath her. Leah stares at the three shining bullets I pull out, holding the pebbles of death in my palm. Her gaze doesn't stray as I reload the gun, closing the chamber before checking the safety is still off.

Then, I offer it to her.

She stares at me like I'm a mad woman.

"If you want to kill yourself, this is your last chance."

"I don't understand," she stutters.

"It's not going to be easy. You're not cured. Hell, I doubt either of us ever will be. Despite everything we went through, I still believe there is a God out there. We've been reunited for a reason."

Leah tentatively nods. "Me too."

"I'm offering you an out for the last time. This is your final chance."

With the gun in one hand, I stretch out my empty palm. Leah studies the olive branch, glancing between the two options. She worries her bottom lip with her teeth, still shaking like a leaf.

"I don't want to die," she admits in a timid whisper. "Not like this. I didn't stay afloat for so long just to let myself drown now. I want a life raft." Her eyes meet mine with a flicker of determination. "I want you."

"I've always been yours. I still am."

Leah drags her fingertips down my arm, gulping hard. When her hand lands in mine, ignoring the offered gun, I unleash a smile. Impossibly, she grins right back. There's still pain in her eyes, I think there always will be. But her hand squeezes mine tight.

"I want to taste you," Leah murmurs.

"Uh, what?"

She shoves me, using her whole body weight to throw me

back on the bed. I'm stunned to silence as she grabs my ankles to drag me down, so I'm splayed out across the tangled silk sheets. There's a new air of confidence in her movements, even with blood and come still staining her skin.

Leah grabs the knife, testing its weight in her hand. When her eyes look up to mine, I swear the Devil is staring back at me. Muddied lake water has transformed into the glistening jewels of a tropical ocean, brimming with excitement. She's never touched me like this before. I've always topped, even as kids.

"Hold still, mistress," she orders crisply.

Hand clenched around the knife, Leah slices through the PVC of my dress like butter. Peeling the two halves of fabric away, she exposes my bare body to her gaze. I'm wearing nothing but tattoos and perfume. Her eyes greedily eat me up, noting the floral design I had inked to cover scars on my hips.

Her finger traces one. "You cut yourself?"

"I used to, before I started this job."

"Why?"

Staring at the ceiling, I find the truth. "Control."

Splaying her right hand across my belly, Leah eases my legs open. It feels unnatural to be so exposed and vulnerable. I'm never the one receiving, it's always been too triggering for me. I like the power. But with her...I make myself relax and submit.

"I used to touch myself late at night while thinking about your lips on my pussy," she reveals.

I fist the bed sheets as she runs a finger over the seam of my soaked cunt, teasing me. Her thumb swirls over my clit, briefly pinching and making my back arch off the bed.

"Nobody goes down on me," I offer back.

"Never?"

"Not once."

Pure, primal possession shines in her eyes.

"I'm glad that I will be the first."

I take a deep breath as her lips meet my pussy, her tongue darting out to slip between my folds. It feels alien at first, but as she begins to find her rhythm, I relax into it. Just seeing my fallen angel naked, bloody, and crouched between my legs like that... *fuck*.

There are no words.

Her finger eases inside my slit, tentative and exploratory. My nails dig into the bed sheets, unused to someone else's touch on my skin. I'm more familiar with burying a vibrator in myself when the need arises. I get off on torturing others more than anything. My legs begin to close around Leah's head, and she lets out an annoyed growl.

"Stop running, you can be vulnerable with me," she chastises.

"It's not that—"

"Shut the fuck up, Ariel. If you're going to make me live in this shitty life, I expect you to compensate. I want to be the one in control too. You're going to learn to live with that."

"Leah—"

Cursing again, her lips vanish as she climbs to her feet. I'm left alone on the bed, listening to the soft pad of her footsteps heading for the dresser. When Leah returns, there's a familiar black gag clasped in her hands. I raise a single eyebrow.

"Not a chance."

"You think I'm giving you a choice?" she returns hotly.

I don't realise the gun is back in her hands until she points it straight at me. With the tables turned, I'm left a little dizzy. The power is firmly back in her hands. Even if it is uncomfortable, seeing this new side of Leah is worth experiencing a taste of my own medicine. I hold still as she slips the ball in my mouth, fastening the gag behind my head.

"Lay back down and spread your legs."

Unable to argue, I decide to humour her and do as instructed. The gag is painful in my mouth but being silenced is surprisingly hot. I never expected to enjoy a role reversal, though I doubt I would if it were anyone but her.

Still holding the gun, Leah sits between my legs. She lazily strokes herself while studying me, tweaking a lace-covered nipple before dipping her hand back between her legs.

"I'm wet again," she observes. "Huh."

Glancing down at the gun in her hand, I spot the moment an idea strikes her. Leah checks to make sure the safety is on before grabbing the lubricant from the bedside table. I watch as she covers the barrel of the gun, probably damaging it in the process, though its purpose has now changed.

With a smirk that steals my breath, she drags the gun over my pussy lips in a teasing move. My heart is hammering at full speed, warmth gathering between my legs already. When the gun slowly pushes inside of me, I gasp around the ball gag. It's freezing cold and the metal bites into my flesh, heightening the feeling.

"I want to make you come with this gun," Leah marvels. "I've carried this thing around every night for the past week, waiting for the perfect moment. I wanted to use it. Fuck, did I want to."

Using the gun like a sex toy, she slowly fucks me with it. My chest rumbles with pleasure, not a single sound able to escape. The wildness of this moment has an orgasm already licking at my insides, fuelled further by her thumb returning to my clit.

"You've taken that power from me," she concludes. "But given me something else. This right here…this is power. I want to do what you do. I want to make people beg and hurt. I want control."

Quickening her movements, she grins evilly as my release starts to crest. I fist the sheets even harder, a little unnerved by the fact that someone else is making me come for the first time ever.

I've never given anyone that level of ownership, only her. She's stolen my soul and dragged it to the depths of hell for her own amusement.

"Let go," she commands. "I want to see what it looks like."

When she pinches my clit painfully, I allow myself to shatter.

My climax takes over, flushing heat through my whole body, contrasting the cold gun still buried deep inside of me. Leah keeps going, drinking in all the details.

"You're right. It is beautiful."

When I finally come down and collapse on the bed, she extricates the gun. Now we've both been marked by the weapon intended to end her life. It feels fitting somehow that it should bring us back together, the very thing that would have ripped us apart forever.

Leah curls up beside me, gently unfastening the gag. She pulls it from my mouth and tosses the contraption aside. Flexing my aching jaw, I pull in a deep, unsteady breath.

"Damn, wildflower. That was the hottest thing I've ever seen."

She frowns. "Me getting you off?"

I stroke my hand along her jaw. "You being empowered."

Her leg slings across mine, pulling us flush against each other. There's nothing left between us now, no storm threatening to drag us apart. All is said and done. We've bloodied and bruised the other. The shadows in her eyes remain, but there's something else there now.

I think it's hope.

She can see the fork in the road.

I'll drag her down the right path.

"I'll teach you everything, if that's what you want," I offer. "This kind of work isn't for everyone. I won't lie and pretend there isn't a cost."

Leah nods decisively. "I have never felt so alive. When your hands were around my throat, I thought that was it." She pauses, considering her words. "I want to be worshipped like God. I want the power."

Our foreheads meet automatically.

"I will always worship you, my wildflower. I never stopped."

CHAPTER
SIX

LEAH

THE SHORE WASHES over our bare feet. Light spring
sunshine has warmed the freezing air, offering some respite. We
waited until the moon was high in the sky to light our path
down to the beach.

Not a soul disturbs our peace.

We're alone, like ghosts lost in the dark.

Ariel begins to pull off her clothing. I follow suit, stripping
down to my underwear. We're both shivering, but neither one of
our smiles abates. Linking hands without saying a word, we
stride deeper into the sea. Water laps at my calves, thighs, hips.
Deeper and deeper.

"Time to swim," Ariel declares.

With broad strokes, she takes the lead. I follow her,
swimming awkwardly with the gun clasped in my hand. It takes
a while to make it far out into the waves, calm and steady.

The further we swim, the quieter it becomes. The world
revolves around the two of us, lost in the night. We both stop,
treading water to stay afloat in the ocean.

Ariel reaches out to tuck soaking wet hair behind my ear. She
insisted I carry the gun, given its significance. This is my burden
to shed, once and for all. It's heavy and fully loaded this time.

"Are you ready?" she asks.

Legs kicking, I grin at her. "I'm ready."

"Then let go. You don't need an escape route anymore."

Holding the weight of the gun, I squeeze the weapon as you would a lover's outstretched hand. This was supposed to be my salvation. The end of my struggles. One well-placed bullet and I'd receive the Lord's mercy after fighting for so long.

I'm not sure how, but this evil creature has flicked a switch inside of me. Salvation holds no more appeal. I don't want God's forgiveness. Fuck no. I want his wrath. Rage. Vengeance and hellfire.

I want to shame even the most sinful of demons and make Lucifer himself blush beet red. When I watched that tempting light fade with Ariel's hands at my throat, a decision was made. Heaven can wait. I'm not done with this hellish plane of existence yet.

Silently, I let the gun slip from my hands. It's swallowed by the black depths of the ocean, sinking and disappearing from sight. I don't need to watch it hit the ocean floor.

The strange tugging feeling in my chest is proof enough. I can almost feel my soul sinking with it, content to dance in the comfort of the dark that welcomes us both. The gun disappears and my life begins anew.

"Leah?"

I meet Ariel's violet eyes. "Yes?"

"I'm so fucking proud of you."

We're magnetised together, legs entwining in the water. Lips meeting in a savage clash, we battle to consume the other in the light of the moon that witnessed our reunion. When we break apart, both panting, the crash of waves returns again.

"I lied," I blurt.

Her eyebrows pull together. "What are you talking about?"

"Back at St Lucien's, nine years ago. I lied to you."

"Leah—"

"I love you. I always have. Then and now."

Without missing a beat, Ariel crushes her mouth to mine again. I don't care about staying afloat in this moment. I'll drown happily. Gladly. Willingly. As long as her heart remains with mine in the afterlife.

"I love you, wildflower. Then and now."

We stare at each other with something that feels a lot like happiness. I'm not naive. I know we will have struggles to come. The darkness never truly abates for people like us. But she's right. I won't swim against the current any longer. It can sweep me along, with Ariel by my side.

"Come on." Her hand takes mine. "We have a client to prepare for. Tonight, my apprentice, you're in charge. May God help us."

"We don't need his help. Not anymore. We make our own luck now."

Ariel nods her approval. "A-fucking-men to that."

The End

AFTERWORD

Thank you for reading *Drown in You*.

Ariel & Leah may return in the future.
For now, they have their happy ending.

Want to read more like this?
Check out my other books on Amazon!

ABOUT THE AUTHOR

J Rose is an independent dark romance author from the United Kingdom. She writes challenging, plot-driven stories packed full of angst, heartbreak and broken characters fighting for their happily ever afters.

Feel free to reach out on social media, J Rose loves talking to her readers!

For exclusive insights, updates, and general mayhem, join J Rose's Bleeding Thorns on Facebook.

Enquiries: j_roseauthor@yahoo.com

Come join the chaos. Stalk J Rose here…
www.jroseauthor.com/socials

NEWSLETTER

Want more madness? Sign up to J Rose's newsletter for monthly announcements, exclusive content, sneak peeks, giveaways and more!

www.jroseauthor.com/newsletter

ALSO BY J ROSE

Buy Here:

www.jroseauthor.com/books

Blackwood Institute

Twisted Heathens

Sacrificial Sinners

Desecrated Saints

Sabre Security

Corpse Roads

Skeletal Hearts

Hollow Veins

Standalones

Forever Ago

Drown in You

Writing as Jessalyn Thorn

Departed Whispers

Printed in Great Britain
by Amazon

42319045R00046